MOUSE HOUSE

TAHIR SHAH

KOK KAR YING

MOUSE HOUSE

TAHIR SHAH

KOK KAR YING

MMXXIII

Secretum Mundi Publishing Ltd
124 City Road
London
EC1V 2NX
United Kingdom

www.secretum-mundi.com
info@secretum-mundi.com

First published by Secretum Mundi Publishing Ltd in
Daydreams of an Octopus & Other Stories, 2022
Published in this edition, 2023

MOUSE HOUSE

Artwork drawn by Kok Kar Ying

A CIP catalogue record for this title is available from the British Library.

ISBN 978-1-914960-90-1

VERSION 02052023

Visit the author's website:
Tahirshah.com

Once upon a time, long ago, when it was said the great mountains were no taller than molehills, a kingdom more lush and verdant than any other lay beyond the rivers and the seas.

The name of that land was Waliaq, which in the local language meant 'a place of blissful radiance'. Never has a realm been so aptly named, for Waliaq was perfect in every way.

In the fields the farmers tended crops, their oxen healthier than can be described. In the markets, the wares on sale were of the finest quality. No one went hungry, and education was free to one and all.

The reason for the kingdom's prosperity
was that the kindest and wisest of kings sat
on the throne. Hailing from an ancestral
line, he thought of others rather than of
himself, and was beloved.

For three-score years,
the wise king ruled over Waliaq.
And in all the days and weeks, months
and years, the populace was as content
as content can be.

Every one of them would praise
their monarch, lauding him for
thinking of them rather than himself.

On the rare occasions that news filtered into the kingdom from neighbouring lands, the people of Waliaq thanked providence for their good fortune.

Unlike the blessed kingdom in which they lived, every nearby realm was ruled by a tyrant, each one crueller than the last.

One morning in early spring, the king
woke from a dream, his head clouded,
his hands trembling. Perceiving something
was wrong, the queen called the vizier,
and he sent for the physician.

An hour later, the monarch was examined.
'What's troubling our beloved ruler?'
asked the queen.

The doctor's expression was grave. 'I regret to say that His Majesty has been afflicted by a malady that medicine cannot cure.'

Letting out a shrill gasp, the queen reached out for her husband's hand. 'If you are unable to cure my husband, then find someone who can!' she cried.

From that moment on, everyone in the kingdom searched for somebody to cure the monarch's malady.

The children in the
schools paused from their studies.
The farmers in the fields ceased their toil.
Even the soldiers on the frontier
halted their guard.

Every mouth in the kingdom
was asking the same question:
'Who can relieve the royal condition?'

Now, it just so happened that a carpenter
who went by the name Blue Green Blue
was passing through on his way to a
neighbouring kingdom on the far
side of the Sleek Mountains.

He was taking refreshment in a teahouse in the capital when he overheard the question on every tongue – how to cure the king's condition.

Intrigued, the carpenter,
Blue Green Blue, asked for details.

'His Majesty's head is clouded,' said one.
'His hands are trembling,' uttered a second.
'He's not himself,' intoned a third.

Curious by nature, Blue Green Blue made his way to the palace gates and, before he knew it, he was admitted into the royal apartment.

In more usual circumstances he may have
been asked for proof of medical ability which,
of course, the carpenter did not possess.
But these were no ordinary times.

An hour after his arrival, having made a study of the patient, Blue Green Blue requested a private audience with the queen.

'I can cure your husband,' the carpenter said.
The queen clasped her hands
together in expectation.
'What will you need?' she asked.

‘A few pieces of wood, some nails,
glue, and a little paint.’
‘I don’t understand,’ the queen intoned.
‘My husband is afflicted with a malady
and needs medicine.’

The carpenter regarded Her Majesty. 'Treatments come in all forms,' he answered. 'And I believe the most effective cure for His Majesty is not an obvious one.'

With no other choices left, it was decided to provide the materials requested for the unconventional treatment.

As soon as he had been given what he needed,
the carpenter locked himself away and worked.

Through days and nights he toiled…
hammering, banging, and creating…

On the other side of the locked door, the queen and the vizier listened, wondering whether they had been taken for fools.

Just as their concern peaked, there was
the sound of a key turning in the lock.

The door opened.

In its frame was standing Blue Green Blue.
And in his hands was a box.

“‘What’s that for?’ asked the queen.
‘It’s the treatment,’ answered the carpenter.

'How has a box ever been a treatment before?'
the vizier quizzed.
Blue Green Blue swallowed hard.

'Who is to say that a treatment must
have been used previously?'
'You mean it's experimental?'
the queen gasped.
'You will have to wait and see,'
spoke Blue Green Blue.

With the king's condition deteriorating by the hour, the carpenter and his box were admitted into the royal bedchamber.

The curtains were drawn shut and
candles were positioned all around.
Only then was the box placed on a
low table beside the royal bed.

There was nothing remarkable about it.
Not at first glance, anyway.
Fashioned from wood, it was painted
in a harlequin design, with a brass motif
of a mouse fixed to the top.

On making an inspection, the vizier and the queen failed to notice that a series of hinges were concealed along the edges of the box. Indeed, they failed to appreciate that all manner of complexities might be hidden inside.

The carpenter asked for a large candelabra
to be brought closer, to provide adequate
illumination for the device.

'*Device*?' questioned the queen. 'How can this be a device? It looks like a silly box, the kind that's given to children to amuse them.'

Blue Green Blue smiled
through the corner of his mouth.
'You will see, Your Highness,' he said.

A crystal candelabra was brought near, shadows festooning the silk-covered walls. Propped up in bed against a mass of pillows, the king stared blankly into space.

He hadn't responded to anything, or to anyone, in many weeks. And now that the royal bedchamber was lost in shadow, the lids began drooping over his eyes.

Seizing the moment, the carpenter took a step backwards, bowed towards the bedstead, and whispered:
'If it pleases Your Majesty, I shall begin.'

The queen and the vizier looked on.
Neither appeared at all impressed.
Indeed, they were both bristling.

But before either could voice disapproval,
the carpenter fumbled in his coat pocket
and removed something…

White and wriggly, it was a live mouse.

Blue Green Blue plucked a little
silver whistle from his lapel pocket,
put it to his lips, and blew.

The sound was so high-pitched as to be almost unheard by human ears.

The creature scurried down the carpenter's arm, then leapt onto the nightstand upon which the wooden harlequin box was sitting. Appearing to stand to attention, it paused there, bathed in the candlelight.

Beyond the bedstead, the vizier
and the queen watched, each aghast.
The carpenter blew the whistle a
second time, more forcefully.
As though commanded to begin,
the mouse scurried forwards.

Climbing up onto the top of the box,
the little creature reached out with both
paws and pressed them into the eyes
of the brass mouse motif.
A moment passed.

Then, a pleasing melody began to play.
As it filled the royal bedchamber,
the sides of the harlequin box lowered.

A moment after that, an intricate mechanism opened out, powered by clockwork coils and springs.

The mouse apparently knew what to do. Without wasting a moment, it scurried down a little chute, whizzing and whirling through the mechanism.

'What is going on?!' snapped the vizier.
Blue Green Blue held a finger to his lips.
The mouse scurried faster and faster,
its miniature form blurred.

The faster it moved, the more the
mechanism moved around it.
And the more the mechanism moved,
the more wondrous it became.

At first it had appeared a dull silver-grey.
But as the mouse careened down the chutes,
along the coils and through the hinged flaps,
the device began to glow.

One moment it was iridescent yellow.
The next it was the deepest shade of blue.
Then, ruby red, emerald, topaz,
and burnt sienna.

The mouse and the machinery around it were so captivating that the queen and the vizier failed to notice its effect.

For between where they were standing and the
harlequin box, the royal patient was stirring.
All of a sudden, his eyes opened wide.
He let out a great exhalation, as though
miraculously cured.

Within a week, the king had regained his strength and order was returned to the Kingdom of Waliaq.

Celebrations rang through the streets
and continued through days and nights.
Every man, woman, and child rejoiced
that their beloved monarch had been
restored to perfect health.

The harlequin box, known within the royal apartment as the 'Mouse House', was taken to the vaults.

Kept under guard, it was deemed to be the most important treasure in the entire kingdom.

As for the carpenter, Blue Green Blue,
he was given a grand title and a fitting pension.

Time passed.

The king grew advanced in years. And, as so often happens in the realms of both folklore and reality, a reign of calm gave way to terror.

The great Kingdom of Waliaq was overrun by brigands from the north. Within days of their arrival, every gold coin had been confiscated, and every young man enslaved.

The king and his family were banished,
their palace razed to the ground.
As for the treasure vaults,
they were picked clean.

Made of wood as it was, the Mouse House
was kicked onto the ground and forgotten.
Rampaging through the streets,
the brigands eventually moved on.

A century and a half slipped by.

The Kingdom of Waliaq no longer existed as it had once done. A lost memory, the region was all but deserted, having never recovered from the attack.

One day, a dervish was wandering across the landscape when he happened upon the ruined city. Making his way up to where the palace of the wise king had once stood, he descended a flight of steep steps and found himself in the vault.

The vault had, of course, been stripped bare of its contents long before. With the advance of years, a lattice of twisting vines covered the walls and floor.

As the seeker looked around,
something caught his eye.
A wooden box.

The colours a little more faded than they
had once been, it was lying on its side,
like a child's discarded toy.

Reaching down, the dervish picked it up and weighed it in his hands. He took in the harlequin pattern and the curious brass motif of a mouse on the top.

Although his order regarded possessions as superfluous to human needs, the seeker was unable to leave the object where it was, for it was as though his journey had at last been given purpose.

Wrapping the box in a cloth,
he set out to the distant place
where the dervish order was based.

For weeks he travelled.
Over mountains and across deserts.
Through forests and along rivers.
Until he reached the valley.

Once fed and rested, the seeker called the other members of the order to cluster around. Choosing his words with care, he explained what had taken place.

And then, untying the cloth,
he revealed the wooden box.

One at a time, the dervishes inspected the object, wondering out loud what it could be.

'It's very sacred,' said the first.
'And ancient,' a second broke in.
'We must worship it,' uttered a third.

So, a special niche was made in a cave wall, and the harlequin box was positioned on a nest of crystals from the bed of the lake.

All day and all night, the dervishes gave prayers for the mysterious box and thanked divine forces for blessing them with such an object.

Once in a while, one of the order would ask what the box was for. But as soon as such a question was voiced, it was shouted down.

As the centuries passed, the box became the centre of the order itself. Dervishes would journey from distant lands merely to be in the presence of such a revered object.

A complex liturgy was developed by which to revere the box, and an entire body of sacred testaments was written to laud it.

Never once was the box
removed from the niche.

Not until a cold spring morning, when
one of the young dervishes had a dream.
He dreamt that the harlequin box was
not trapped in the niche, but was set free…
free on the ocean.

Tasked with praying over the sacred box in the dead of night, the young dervish prised it out of the niche and hurried away.

At dawn, the theft was discovered.
Bells rang out through the valley.
The dervish order descended into a
state of terror – a terror from which
they never recovered.

The young dervish carried the box over mountains, through forests, and across deserts. Eventually, he reached the shores of the ocean.

Whispering a blessing, the dervish hurled the box into the waves.

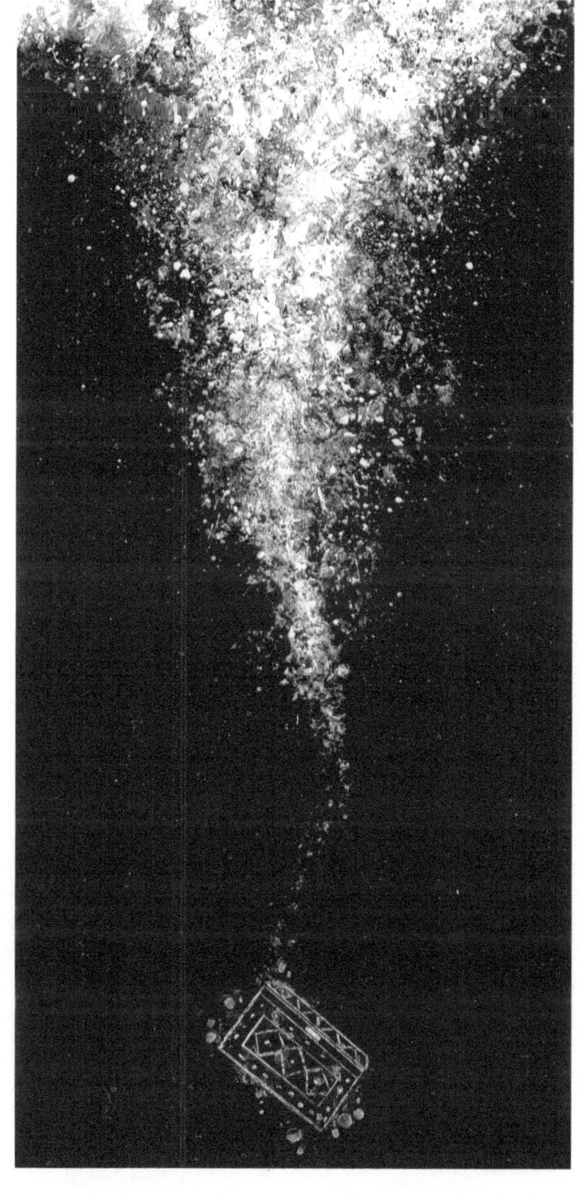

Fashioned so long before by
Blue Green Blue, the box bobbed
up and down on the ocean swell.

Storms ravaged it.
The sun baked it.
The brine bleached the colour from its wood.
Still, though, the box bobbed up and down…

Until, one bright summer evening, it was caught in the net of a little trawler fishing off the island of Sulawesi.

Assuming it to be some kind of container, the captain of the vessel took it to his cabin. Despite trying for hours on end, he simply couldn't manage to open the box.

A few days passed,
and the trawler reached port.

Once on dry land, the captain carried the box into the town and sold it for next to nothing. As so often happens, it was traded over and over, zigzagging from stall to stall and from shop to shop.

In the following months, it was thought to be a child's toy, a drum, an expression of art, and even an aspidistra stand.

No one had any idea of the history of the box.
But the more mysterious it was considered
to be, the more its price rose.

A year and a day after being trapped in the fishing net, the box found its way to an exclusive gallery on London's St. James's Street, where it was displayed on a special marble plinth.

An accompanying description in
small black type described it as
An important Shang Dynasty meditation box.
The guide price was £722,950.

As chance would have it, the wife of an American billionaire was passing the gallery when she spied the box sitting on its plinth. So enamoured was she with the object – which appeared to have no conventional use at all – that she bought it right there on the spot.

£323,000
£722,950

A week later, she presented it to her husband, who was charmed. He liked it so much that he had it placed on a stand in his bedroom.

A decade passed.

Then another.

Then, one morning, the billionaire was shaving when he fell to the bathroom floor. Tests were done, and he was diagnosed as having had a 'cryptogenic stroke'.

Unable to talk, move, or communicate in
any way, he lay propped up in bed,
his gaze fixed on the curious box.

Days slipped into weeks, then months…

The greatest minds of the medical
world examined the patient.
One by one, they spouted excuses,
took their fees, and shuffled away.

Early one summer morning, a nurse
opened the curtains and then the windows.
As dazzling sunshine streamed in, the
patient was propped up on a mound of
goose-feather pillows.

Then, while the nurse bustled out of the room, a little brown field mouse scurried in through the open window and across the floor.

Unobserved and without a sound,
it scampered up the stand and
onto the antique box.

At that very moment, the patient's wife stepped out into the gardens with her dogs. Fishing a little silver whistle from her pocket, she blew it twice.

The field mouse stood to attention.

Then, as though programmed to do so,
it reached forwards and pressed its paws in
the eyes of the now well-worn mouse motif.
A pleasing melody filled the room.

As it did so, the box's intricate mechanism opened out. The little brown field mouse slipped down the chute and began whizzing and whirling amid the coils and springs. Within a minute, the sides of the box closed up again.

The patient wide awake, the little field mouse scurried out into the garden.

In the years since, the billionaire has given away almost his entire fortune to good causes.

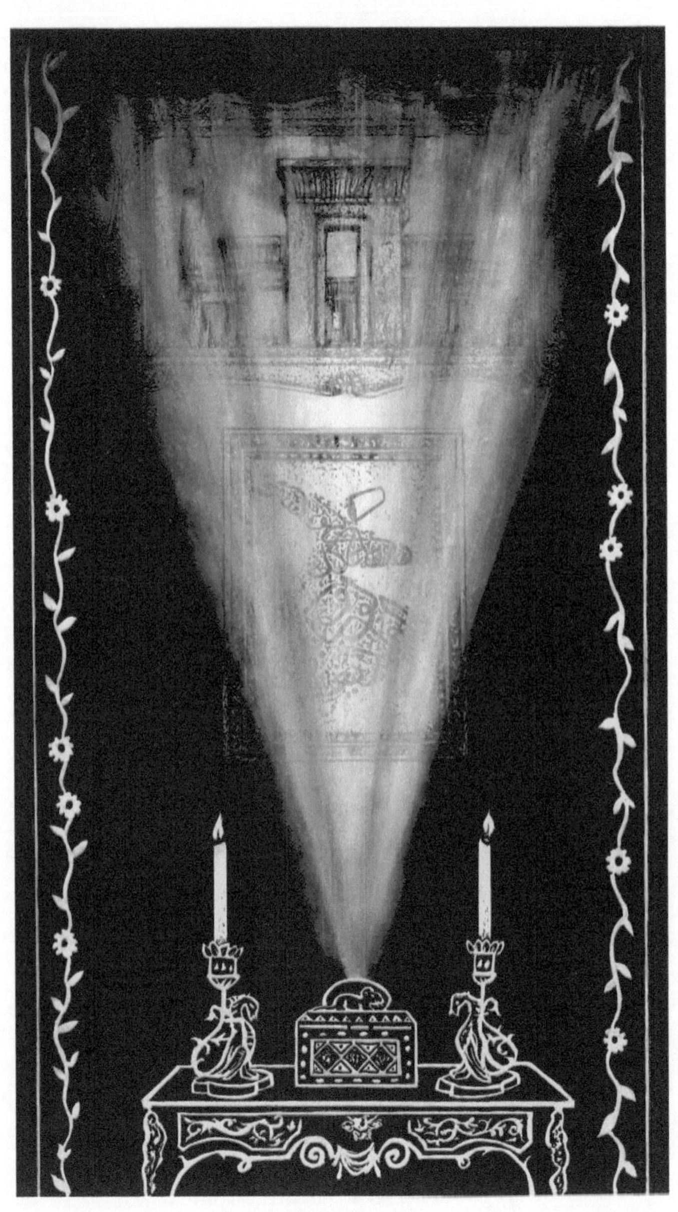

As for the Mouse House,
it's still there in his bedroom,
awaiting its next adventure.

Finis

About the Author

Descended from a long line of storytellers, writers, and savants, Tahir Shah is one of the most prolific authors of his generation. He has published more than sixty books in numerous genres, including travel, fiction, and fantasy, as well as tales for children.

Raised in the tradition of Eastern 'teaching stories', Shah is passionate about stories and storytelling. He regards the ability to learn from folklore as being in us all, what he calls a 'default setting of humankind'. As well as having written scores of books, Shah has made documentaries for National Geographic TV and The History Channel. He is the founder and CEO of the charity, The Scheherazade Foundation.

About the Artist

Kok Kar Ying is a passionate illustrator from Malaysia who creates art by adapting and experimenting with a variety of traditional and digital media. Her aim is to bring authors' words to life with creative compositions and highly detailed artworks. She has experience in illustrating children's books and educational materials.

Books By Tahir Shah

Travel

Trail of Feathers
Travels With Myself
Beyond the Devil's Teeth
In Search of King Solomon's Mines
House of the Tiger King
In Arabian Nights
The Caliph's House
Sorcerer's Apprentice
Journey Through Namibia

Novels

Jinn Hunter: Book One – The Prism
Jinn Hunter: Book Two – The Jinnslayer
Jinn Hunter: Book Three – The Perplexity
Hannibal Fogg and the Supreme Secret of Man
Hannibal Fogg and the Codex Cartographica
Casablanca Blues
Eye Spy
Godman
Paris Syndrome
Timbuctoo

Nasrudin

Travels With Nasrudin
The Misadventures of the Mystifying Nasrudin
The Peregrinations of the Perplexing Nasrudin
The Voyages and Vicissitudes of Nasrudin
Nasrudin in the Land of Fools

Teaching Stories

The Arabian Nights Adventures
Scorpion Soup
Tales Told to a Melon
The Afghan Notebook
The Caravanserai Stories
Ghoul Brothers
Hourglass
Imaginist
Jinn's Treasure
Jinnlore
Mellified Man
Skeleton Island
Wellspring
When the Sun Forgot to Rise
Outrunning the Reaper
The Cap of Invisibility
On Backgammon Time
The Wondrous Seed
The Paradise Tree
Mouse House
The Hoopoe's Flight
The Old Wind
A Treasury of Tales
Daydreams of an Octopus & Other Stories

Miscellaneous

The Reason to Write
Zigzag Think
Being Myself

Research

Cultural Research

The Middle East Bedside Book

Three Essays

Anthologies

The Anthologies

The Clockmaker's Box

The Tahir Shah Fiction Reader

The Tahir Shah Travel Reader

Edited by

Congress With a Crocodile

A Son of a Son, Volume I

A Son of a Son, Volume II

Screenplays

Casablanca Blues: The Screenplay

Timbuctoo: The Screenplay

A REQUEST

If you enjoyed this book, please review it on your favourite online retailer or review website.

Reviews are an author's best friend.

To stay in touch with Tahir Shah, and to hear about his upcoming releases before anyone else, please sign up for his mailing list:

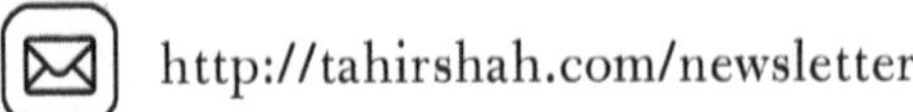

http://tahirshah.com/newsletter

And to follow him on social media, please go to any of the following links:

http://www.twitter.com/humanstew

@tahirshah999

http://www.facebook.com/TahirShahAuthor

http://www.youtube.com/user/tahirshah999

http://www.pinterest.com/tahirshah

https://www.goodreads.com/tahirshahauthor

http://www.tahirshah.com

www.ingramcontent.com/pod-product-compliance
Lightning Source LLC
Chambersburg PA
CBHW030521310726
48979CB00010B/1757/J